SPACE TAXI

WATER
PLANET
RESCUE

WITHDRAWN

By Wendy Mass and Michael Brawer

Illustrated by Elise Gravel

LITTLE, BROWN AND COMPANY
New York   Boston

Copyright © 2014 by Wendy Mass and Michael Brawer
Illustrations copyright © 2014 by Elise Gravel

Little, Brown and Company

Hachette Book Group
1290 Avenue of the Americas, New York, NY 10104
Visit us at lb-kids.com

Little, Brown and Company is a division of Hachette Book Group, Inc.
The Little, Brown name and logo are trademarks of Hachette Book Group, Inc.

The publisher is not responsible for websites (or their content) that are not owned by the publisher.

First Paperback Edition: March 2015
First published in hardcover in September 2014 by Little, Brown and Company

Library of Congress Cataloging-in-Publication Data

Mass, Wendy, 1967–
Water planet rescue / by Wendy Mass and Michael Brawer ; illustrations by Elise Gravel. — First edition.
    pages cm — (Space taxi)
    ISBN 978-0-316-24323-0 (hardcover) — ISBN 978-0-316-24322-3 (paperback) —
ISBN 978-0-316-24325-4 (ebook) — ISBN 978-0-316-24336-0 (library edition ebook) [1. Interplanetary voyages—Fiction. 2. Adventure and adventurers—Fiction. 3. Fathers and sons—Fiction.]
    I. Brawer, Michael. II. Gravel, Elise, illustrator. III. Title.
    PZ7.M42355Wat 2014
    [Fic]—dc23
                                        2013044221

10 9 8 7 6 5 4

LSC-C

Printed in the United States of America

Dedicated to our giant cat, Bubba,
the inspiration for Pockets.
He's not as smart as Pockets, though.
And the only thing he can hide in his fur
is more fur.

CONTENTS

Chapter One:
Cats Don't Swim

I know everyone thinks their family is strange, but seriously, mine has them all beat. First of all, my dad drives a taxi in OUTER SPACE! Second of all, *I'm* somehow able to read the space map that helps him get from planet to planet. And third, since my little sister, Penny, only eats things that start with the letter *P*, I had to eat a persimmon for dessert last night. A persimmon is kind of like a cross between a mango and a tomato, only not as good as either a mango or a tomato. I asked Mom why we couldn't have popcorn (also starts with a *P*) instead, but she said if she has to pop one more batch of popcorn, she's going to run screaming through the neighborhood in her nightgown.

See? I told you. Weird family!

But I haven't even gotten to the weirdest part yet. A few days ago we got a talking cat from another planet. Pockets helps protect the universe as an Intergalactic Security Force officer. We call him Pockets because he can fit almost anything into pockets hidden behind patches of fur on his belly. And also his real name is way too long to remember.

Pockets made Dad and me deputies of the Intergalactic Security Force (called the ISF for short) because we helped him catch a criminal and sort of save the universe at the same time.

The ISF needs Dad to be available whenever Pockets has a mission for us, so his regular space taxi job is on hold awhile. I had expected Dad to grumble about this because he loves driving his taxi, but nope. He's totally into being home all the time. Two days ago he fixed that crack in the wall in our kitchen (but made a new one on the floor by dropping a brick). Then he painted the family room green (and dripped paint all over Mom's favorite chair), and tried to put up a shelf but only made two really big holes in the wall, which Mom had to cover with an old, broken clock.

Yesterday he took us to the zoo, where Penny got scared by the butterfly exhibit and cried until we got kicked out for upsetting the other kids. Today we're going swimming. Hopefully nothing will go wrong at the pool, but the odds are against it.

Truthfully? I'm itching to get back to outer space, and I *know* Mom is ready for Dad to get back to work.

"Got your suit on, Archie?" Dad calls out from the hall. "The pool opens in half an hour."

"Coming!" I grab my ISF badge and

my space map and tuck them into my pool bag. ISF deputy Archie Morningstar is ALWAYS ready for duty. Mom said she'll only let me do this job if I promise to look before I leap and always listen to Dad and Pockets. She says I don't "think things through," because of one trip (okay, *four* trips) to the principal's office last year due to a series of science projects that didn't work out as expected. The janitor was able to get the scorch marks off the ceiling after only a few weeks of scrubbing, so really, I don't see what all the fuss was about.

When I get to the living room I spot Pockets asleep in his favorite sunny spot on the window ledge. That cat sure sleeps a lot. And he sheds a TON. Our apartment is covered in clumps of white fur. It sticks to the carpet and hangs from the walls (still wet from the paint) and lampshades and furniture. I don't know how one cat can shed so much. Mom's vacuum cleaner is lying on the floor, broken. Clearly, it was no match for all this fur.

You wouldn't know it from all the shedding, but Pockets likes things to be neat and orderly. He cleans up my room every time I leave it. I haven't told Mom yet that it's not my doing. She'll figure it out soon enough.

"This is NOT what I signed up for," a voice growls from behind me. I turn around to see Pockets frowning up at me, his paws on his hips. He's wearing a pair of my old yellow swim trunks and Penny's purple goggles. I turn back to look at the

TODAY iN FELiNE FASHION

window ledge, where I can swear I'm looking at Pockets asleep, then back again to
the cat behind me. I rub my eyes to make
sure I'm fully awake.

"If you're here," I ask him as my dad
walks into the room, "then who's that
sleeping by the window? Do you have a

twin? Can you clone yourself?" Do I now have TWO talking pet cats?

Dad strides across the room and pokes at the sleeping cat on the ledge. His finger goes right through! It's not a cloned space cat after all. It's a Pockets-shaped ball of fur! I admit I'm a little disappointed.

Dad lifts up the huge pile of fur. "This," he announces, "is the sign of a cat who needs a good grooming."

"How do we know that's mine?" Pockets asks, crossing his paws in front of him.

Dad and I raise our eyebrows at him.

"All right, all right," Pockets says, walking toward Dad. "I can't help it. Something in the air on your planet makes my fur grow very quickly." He waves the dangling fluff ball away, and white fur flies in all directions. I sneeze as a few pieces fly up my nose. I consider reminding him that he shed a lot before he even got to Earth, but he looks like he's in kind of a dark mood.

"Can we focus on the larger problem here?" Pockets demands. He points to his swim shorts with one front paw and to his goggles with the other.

Dad turns to me. "I don't see a problem with the way Pockets looks," he says. "Do you, Archie?"

I try hard not to giggle. "He looks like a cat who's ready to go swimming."

Dad nods. "My thoughts exactly, son."

Pockets tries to pull off his goggles, but they just snap back in his face. "I am a highly respected Intergalactic Security Force officer," he says, puffing out his chest.

"I have won medals for bravery on more missions than I can count. But one thing I do NOT do is swim."

"Why not?" I ask.

"Cats don't swim," he replies.

"But why not?" I ask.

"They just don't," he snaps.

Dad puts his arm around Pockets. "We're only fooling with you. Of course you don't have to come. In fact, the pool doesn't allow pets. You were a very good sport to let Penny dress you up this way."

Pockets seems calmed by Dad's words. He shrugs. "No harm, I suppose. The worst part was having to keep my mouth shut."

"I know it's hard pretending to be a regular cat around Penny," Dad says, "but we've been over this. She's too young to keep your secret identity as a crime-fighting cat from outer space. What if she told her friends at preschool? They'd tell their parents, and your cover would be blown."

Personally, I don't think we have to worry about this, because Penny only says, like, three words. And never in a row.

"I understand," Pockets says. "I am a trained professional. I can pretend to be a house pet, easy. See?" He begins to purr and rubs up against Dad's leg like a regular cat. With a swish of his tail, he walks away, leaving a thick coating of white fur behind.

Dad looks down at his fur-covered legs. "Guess we're making a stop on the way to the pool. That cat's getting a haircut!"

CHAPTER TWO:
What's Better Than a Bath?

Pockets's goggles won't come off. They are tangled in his fur. We can't even use scissors without worrying about poking him. I'm sure he has some kind of alien gadget hidden in one of his pockets that would fix it, but since Penny's with us, he just has to wait for the groomer to deal with it.

He basically pouts and growls the whole way there in Dad's taxi until Penny leans out of her car seat and starts to pet him. Then he starts to purr. She kisses him on the head and he rubs against her hand. Mom says Penny could charm the rattles off a snake.

Dad parks around the corner from the groomer's. I unstrap Pockets and half drag, half carry him out of the car. Penny waves good-bye. "Have a nice bath!" Mom calls out her window. As soon as we're out of sight of the car, Pockets springs from my arms. He grabs something the size of a pen from one of his pockets.

"Oomph!" Dad says, banging his face on what looks like thin air. He backs up, then reaches out with his hand to feel in front of him. I reach out, too. My hand hits what feels like a solid wall!

"What's going on here?" Dad asks, knocking on the invisible surface.

I shake my head at Pockets as he casually slips his pen-like device back into a pocket. "Did you put up an invisible force field?"

Pockets doesn't bother to deny it. "I certainly did! You never said anything about a bath. You know how I feel about water."

Dad rubs his nose. "You're making too big a deal about this. It'll be over before you know it."

"I do not need a bath!" Pockets insists. "I can clean myself just fine." He proceeds to lick his arm repeatedly. Then he stops, coughs, and hacks up a slimy hairball. It plops onto the sidewalk at our feet.

We stare at it. Pockets's cheeks turn red.

I rest my hand on his shoulder. "I'm

pretty sure you don't want to do *that* in front of the next criminal you try to arrest."

Pockets sighs. "Fine. I shall submit to the bath." He begins emptying his pockets. One by one, he thrusts gadgets and gizmos of all sizes and shapes into our arms. Some things I recognize, like rope and a notebook and a compass. But most of it I don't. I glance around to make sure no one on the street can see us.

"Aren't your pockets waterproof?" Dad asks as our arms fill up.

"I don't want to take any chances with your Earth water," Pockets explains. "Who knows what's in it. No offense, of course." Finally, he pulls out two big black bags, and we stuff everything inside.

"The groomer will be very careful while giving you the bath," Dad promises, hefting the bags over his shoulders. "They do this all day."

"*What*?" Pockets asks, his eyes almost popping out of his face. "Someone GIVES ME THE BATH?"

"Of course," Dad says. "That's part of the groomer's job."

Pockets throws up his paws. "That's it! I'm asking my father for a raise the next time I see him!"

He lets me pick him up without further complaint. This time there's no force field keeping us from entering the groomer's, but Dad walks with his hands out in front of us just to make sure.

"That's one fluffy cat you have," the groomer says as I plop Pockets on the counter. "Pockets Morningstar, right?"

"That's right," Dad replies. "He's very excited to be here."

Pockets flexes one paw, revealing five dagger-sharp claws.

The woman's eyes widen. "We'll be taking care of those, don't you worry. We have special scissors for cutting nails."

Pockets looks at me, his eyes pleading. He needs those claws to be the best police cat he can be.

"Um, maybe you shouldn't clip his claws," I tell the groomer. "He needs those to, you know, climb stuff."

The woman frowns. "He doesn't go outside in the city, does he? That's very dangerous for a cat."

I shake my head. "No, but he likes to, um, climb the curtains in our living room."

This is actually true.

She raises her eyebrows. "And you want him to continue doing that?"

Dad steps in now. "Oh, yes. We think it's very good exercise. As you can see, he could stand to lose a few pounds."

Pockets shoots Dad a look, and I allow myself a giggle.

"Suit yourself," she says, and slides some forms across the counter for Dad to sign. "He'll be ready in an hour. But you can pick him up anytime before five." Then she scoops up Pockets and they disappear behind a curtain. A trail of white fur is all that's left of him.

I don't talk much on the way to the community center, where the indoor pool is located. I can't help feeling kind of bad leaving him there while the rest of us are going to have fun swimming.

Only a few other families are at the pool. Dad tosses colorful plastic hoops into the deep end and I swim down and get them. I wish I could dive in, but I've never been able to do it without landing on my belly. Mom

and Penny are splashing around in the shallow end. Penny loves putting her hand up to the water jets and laughs as the force of the water pushes her hand away. That girl may not talk, but she sure can laugh.

I join them for a few minutes, and Penny and I play a game to see who can keep their hand in front of the jet the longest. She always wins.

I swim back to the deep end. I can't stop thinking about Pockets and how sad he looked. "Think he's okay at the groomer's?" I ask Dad as I hand a red hoop up to him.

"I'm sure he's fine," Dad says. "You heard him. He's had adventures all across the universe. He can handle getting a haircut."

I'm about to swim under for the next ring when a blur running alongside the pool catches my eye.

The blur skids to a stop. Water and bubbles fly everywhere.

It's Pockets! He's still wearing Penny's purple goggles. Soap bubbles cling to his fur in wet clumps. Dad grabs for the watch that he placed on the side of the pool, before Pockets can knock it into the water.

"I can't believe it," Dad says. "You broke out of the groomer's?"

"How did you find us?" I ask, kind of impressed. I'm pretty sure no one told him the address of the pool.

Pockets does this head-to-tail shimmying thing. Soapy water flies out in all directions. His fur doesn't look any shorter. "No time to explain, my good deputies. We've got a mission!"

Chapter Three:
Akbar's Floating Rest Stop

One of the perks of being a taxi driver (even a space taxi driver) is that you can always get a ride when you need one. It only takes a few minutes before one of Dad's friends arrives to take Mom and Penny home.

Dad hooks up Penny's car seat in the

back while Mom fusses over me. I know she's not too happy with my new job, but being a copilot is a Morningstar family tradition. You can't argue with tradition.

"Promise you'll be careful up there," she says, hugging me tight. "Do what Dad and Pockets tell you."

I hug her back until Dad honks for me.

I'm so excited that my legs won't stop bouncing in my seat. Or maybe I'm just cold because I'm in a wet bathing suit. Nah, I'm excited! Our first official mission!

"All right, Pockets," Dad says once we're headed toward the airfield. "What's this all about? Start from when we dropped you at the groomer's."

I twist around in my seat and wait for Pockets to answer. He's refilling his pockets with all his gadgets. "It is pretty simple, really," he says. "In the middle of my so-called *bath*, the tiny interlink hidden inside my ear started beeping. It was my father calling from ISF headquarters. He said that the planet Nautilus in the Triangulum Galaxy is experiencing a very strange weather situation. We are the nearest officers, so we're being sent to check it out and file a report."

"You're not making this up just to get out of the bath, are you?" Dad asks. He narrows his eyes at Pockets.

"Of course not," Pockets says. "I'm as disappointed as you are about the bath being cut short." His lips quiver and I know he's trying to hide a smile.

"I'm sure," Dad says.

"How did you find us?" I ask. "I bet it was some supercool locator device that lets you track people down anywhere on the planet with a press of a button, right?"

"Nope," Pockets says, tapping his nose. "Cats have an excellent sense of smell, you know. You should probably bathe more often. No offense."

It's hard not to be offended when someone basically says you stink so bad they could track your scent across town. "Well, *you* don't like baths, either," I remind him.

"I told you," he says. "Cats are self-cleaning."

I glance at his matted, tangled fur. "Is that a leaf stuck to your tail?"

He turns around in circles in his seat, trying to catch his tail, but he can't. I start to laugh, then reach over to pull the leaf off for him.

"Thanks," he grumbles.

"Boys," Dad says. "You can argue about who needs a bath more when we get home. Right now we have to prepare for the mission."

The com line crackles with a call from Home Base. "Morningstar!" the female mouse squeaks. She comes from a planet where mice can talk, and it's her job to keep track of all the space taxis. Dad told me her name is Minerva. He warned me not to call her Minnie for short, though. One of the newer space taxi drivers made the mistake of calling her *Minnie the Mouse*—or *Minnie Mouse* for short. She didn't like being compared to a cartoon character, so she sent the poor guy to pick up a fare on an ice planet where the temperature was two hundred degrees below zero. It took him a week to thaw out.

I can't wait to meet her.

"We have received your information from the ISF," she continues. At the sound

27

of Minerva's squeaky voice, Pockets's ears stand at alert and his nose twitches. "We have cleared the airfield and made arrangements for you to stop at Akbar's Floating Rest Stop on the way to the planet Nautilus. You will get some special mods for your visit there."

"Roger that," Dad says.

The voice continues. "We miss you at Home Base. Some of your usual fares aren't happy about your...ahem, *vacation*."

"Things will be back to business as usual soon, I'm sure," Dad says.

"Are you certain you can trust this... this *cat*?" she asks, unable to hide her dislike. Turns out cats and mice are sworn enemies everywhere in the universe, not just on Earth.

"I can hear you, you know," Pockets calls from the backseat. He has pulled out a towel and is trying to dry his wet, matted fur.

"I trust him," Dad assures her.

"Fine," she snaps. "You are cleared for takeoff. As usual, be careful up there."

"Always am," Dad says. "Morningstar over and out."

The second set of straps pins us to our seats and the taxi speeds up.

"What are mods?" I have to shout over the noise of the engine.

"Modifications," my dad shouts back. "Changes we need to make to the taxi."

I grip the seat as the front tires lift off the ground and we begin to zoom toward the blue sky. I forgot how fast we go at takeoff. I swallow hard and wait to catch my breath before shouting over the roar of the rocket boosters. "Why do you need to change anything? What's wrong with the taxi?"

"Nothing," Dad yells, pulling down on the throttle as we pass through the clouds. "Nautilus is a water planet. Our space taxi will need to become a space submarine."

Underwater Deputy Archie Morningstar has a nice ring to it! "Do you always have to do this when you go to Nautilus?" I ask.

He shakes his head. "I've been to Akbar's for repairs many times, but I've never been to Nautilus."

This surprises me. Hasn't my dad been everywhere? "But I thought your job took you all over the universe."

"The universe is a really big place, Archie," he says as the taxi picks up speed.

"Even after all these years of traveling through it, I've only seen a tiny slice."

I turn to look behind us. The sun is now a small glowing blob as we head out of the solar system.

"This would be a good time to start guiding us to Akbar's," Dad says. "It's orbiting near the outer arm of the Milky Way."

I stowed the tube under the backseat earlier this morning. Pockets hands it to me, and I hurry to unroll the map. Then I stop. What if my being able to read the map was a one-time thing? What if all I see are dots and squiggles again and Dad has to go back to Earth to find a real space taxi copilot?

I guess I'm about to find out. I lay the map open in my lap and hold my breath.

Nothing happens. I focus on the paper, silently begging it to work. A few seconds later the map springs to life, sending stars and planets into the air above my lap.

PHEW!

"Akbar's Floating Rest Stop, please," I say out loud. The map zooms in on a small object out past a triple star system. I scan the area to see the best route. "Okay, Dad. Left past the third red star, then a quick right."

Dad follows my instructions, and we're on our way.

"Good job, Archie," he says.

"So what's the big weather emergency, anyway?" I ask Pockets.

"Nautilus is covered in water," Pockets tells us. "Half the people live under the ocean, and the other half live on islands they built on the surface. But the water level is going down fast. No one knows why. That's what we're going to find out."

"How are we going to do that?" Dad asks.

"Because *I'm* on the case."

Pockets is a very confident cat.

A few minutes later we approach what looks like a gigantic shopping mall floating in space. A huge flashing billboard sticking out of the top announces: AKBAR'S FLOATING REST STOP, FOR ALL YOUR TRAVEL NEEDS. Then underneath, in smaller (but still huge) letters, it says: IF YOU LIVED HERE, YOU'D BE HOME NOW. Then in even smaller (but still really big) letters it says: JUST KIDDING. YOU CAN'T LIVE HERE. BUT STOP BY FOR A VISIT. WE'RE ALWAYS OPEN.

My eyes open wider and wider as we soar past flashing neon signs for the bathrooms, the snack bar, the gift shop, the game room, and, most surprising of all, a Barney's Bagels and Schmear restaurant! All the way out here!

On every side of the huge floating building are long metal arms with hand-like clamps on the ends. Most of the arms have spaceships of different sizes and shapes attached to them. Dad steers the taxi toward an empty pair of metal arms. The arms reach out toward the taxi and clamp onto our front bumper. The taxi gives a small shudder, and then Dad turns off the engine. He flips on the com line. "Salazar Morningstar," he announces. Then adds, "And friends."

"Greetings, Mr. Morningstar," a friendly voice replies. "Please state the purpose of your visit to Akbar's today."

"We have an appointment at Graff's Garage," Dad says.

"Please stay seated," the voice instructs. The taxi begins to glide along the side of the building, and I crane my neck to see out the window. The metal arms are moving us to another spot. One final jolt and we stop. Then two large metal doors slide open and our car is pulled inside the building. When we stop, we're about twenty feet above the ground. A blinking sign announces: WELCOME TO GRAFF'S GARAGE. IF WE CAN'T FIX IT, IT AIN'T BROKE.

"Enjoy your visit," the pleasant voice says. "And don't forget to get a bagel from Barney's on your way out."

Pockets licks his lips and says, "This Barney's location has the best tuna fish sandwich this side of the Milky Way. Yuuuumy!" He rubs his still-damp belly. That cat sure does love his tuna.

"You've been here before, too?" I ask.

"Everyone's been to Akbar's Rest Stop," Pockets replies. "Come, let's get the taxi fixed up so we can get to the tuna!"

"And to Nautilus," I add.

"Yes, of course," Pockets says, but doesn't take his eyes off the sign for Barney's.

I peer out the windshield. We're nowhere near the ground. Before I can warn him, Pockets flings open his door and steps out.

Chapter Four:
Graff's Garage

"Pockets!" I shout, my heart racing. I throw open my door and look all around. I don't see him anywhere.

"Down here," a voice calls out.

Pockets! I whip my head around until I find him standing on a movable sidewalk that runs along the opposite side of the car. He waves as the sidewalk glides him toward a door in the middle of the wall marked GARAGE.

Phew!

Dad chuckles and I realize he's holding on to the back of my bathing suit. "At least you didn't try to climb out your own door," he says, letting go. "The sidewalk's only on the driver's side."

I scramble over and follow Dad out onto the moving walkway. I try not to think about what would have happened if I had hopped out my own door with nowhere to go but the floor far below. Penny would take my bedroom, that's for sure. She would pull down my maps of the city and replace them with pictures of unicorns and fairies and mermaids. I shudder at the thought.

The sidewalk takes us into a large

mechanic's shop loaded with equipment and vehicles. Whirring, beeping, grinding, and banging sounds bounce off the high ceiling. It would look just like any big mechanic's shop at home if it weren't for the fact that the workers all appear to be giant man-size ants with hard black shells and antennae that wave from their heads as they work.

I shrink back. I still have nightmares from dropping an ant farm when I was in kindergarten. It totally wasn't my fault, by the way. The floor was wet from spilled juice, and anyone would have slipped on it. (Although, now that I think of it, the juice may have been my fault.) The tiny ants flew *everywhere*. Mom was picking them out of my hair for days.

The tallest of the ant guys spots us and waves one long arm. He hops off a ladder and slides a wrench into a pocket hanging off his belt. "Sal Morningstar!" he says in exactly the kind of chirpy voice you would think an ant would have, only deeper. "How you doin', man?"

Dad smiles and reaches for one of the guy's four hands. A stream of oozy grease slides onto Dad's hand as they shake. It came right out of the guy's wrist! Up close I can see they aren't really giant ants, only ant-*like*. Turns out the antennae on their heads are tools attached to a hat. They have regular ears on the sides of their heads. Still, I'm sticking close to Dad.

"Good to see you, Graff," Dad says, wiping his grease-smeared hand on his pants. "Been a long time." He puts his other hand on my shoulder. "This is my son, Archie. He's my copilot now."

Graff's large round eyes shine down at me. "Congratulations, young Morningstar. That's a big responsibility."

I force myself to smile, but it comes out kind of shaky. "I know," I say. And then I blurt out, "We save the universe now, too."

Dad stares at me.

I put my hand over my mouth. Oops! Maybe Dad should worry about *me* giving our secrets away, not Penny.

"Anyway," Dad says, quickly changing the subject, "you got the message we were coming?"

"Sure did," Graff says. "We're all ready for you."

43

At that moment Pockets jumps out from behind me, where I didn't even realize he had been crouching. Is he going to yell at me for saying that thing about saving the universe? Or worse yet, fire us? I was really hoping to get a chance to foil some more crimes.

But he runs right past me, leaps onto Graff's shoulders, and tackles him to the ground! Graff yelps in surprise. Clumps of wet fur and sticky grease fly in all directions as they wrestle. I feel like I should probably do something, but I'm so surprised that I can't seem to move.

The two roll around on the ground meow-ing (Pockets) and chirping (Graff). Dad rushes over, shouting at Pockets to stop. But before he reaches them, they stand up, dust themselves off, and start laughing.

Graff clasps Pockets on the shoulder. "You looked a lot better the last time I saw you, young Pilarbing Fangorious!" Graff says, grinning. "What happened to you?"

Pockets tries to smooth himself down, but it doesn't do any good. He really is a mess. Besides his clumpy wet fur, he now has black grease all over him.

Pockets points one paw at Dad. "*He* thought I needed a bath."

"I would definitely agree with that," Graff says, laughing again.

"So," Dad says, scratching his head. "I'm guessing you two know each other?"

Graff nods. A glob of grease squirts out of the joint in his neck. I try not to stare. "I've known Pilarbing since he was a tiny kitten," he explains. "His father is an old friend. Looks like he's got some new friends now."

I feel kind of silly for being scared of Graff just because of how he looks. I clear my throat and say, "We call him Pockets. You know, because of all his pockets?"

Graff grins again. "Makes sense to me. C'mon, Pockets, let's get you cleaned up." He leads a complaining Pockets over to the other end of the room and pushes him through some curtains. We hear the *whoosh* of water, and then some bubbles spill out from under the curtain. A minute later the whirr of a dryer drowns out the sound of the mechanics working. Then out runs Pockets, clean and mostly dry. His fur doesn't look any shorter, though.

Dad looks Pockets up and down. "Couldn't you have given him a haircut while you were at it?"

Graff laughs. "I wouldn't put pointy

scissors anywhere near that cat. He's quicker than he looks."

Pockets twists his head around to admire himself. "Better," he admits. "Now we really need to get the taxi aqua-fitted. Nautilus will surely have lost more water since we left Earth."

"Already taken care of." Graff steps aside to reveal our taxi, parked right behind us. While we were waiting for Pockets to get clean, the other guys must have been working on the car. Can't say that it looks any different, though.

"Wonderful," Dad says, circling the taxi. He must see something I don't.

"You are now able to go underwater," Graff says proudly.

"How deep?" Pockets asks.

Graff rubs his chin. More grease squirts

out. "We're not sure. At some point the pressure of the water will begin to crush the taxi."

"When is that?" Dad asks. "At fifty yards down? Five hundred?"

Graff shrugs. "Somewhere between those two?"

Pockets sighs. "Okay. So what else can it do?"

"Push the blue button on the dashboard. Skis will pop out of the bottom for a water landing," Graff says.

"Nice," Dad says, nodding.

Graff reaches into the backseat of the taxi and hands Pockets a brown bag. "The ISF also requested you stock up on a few things. We packed you a heat sensor and a few other tools."

Pockets peeks into the bag. "A Flirbin Blaster. Excellent."

"What's a Flirbin Blaster?" I ask, leaning over to look.

Pockets closes the bag. "Sorry, that's on a need-to-know basis only."

"Hmph," I reply.

Graff puts his hand on my shoulder, depositing three circles of grease. "Don't feel too bad, young Morningstar. Here, you can have a gadget of your own." He reaches into his tool belt and hands me what looks like a flashlight with a suction cup at the end. I turn it over in my hands. "What is it?"

"It's called an air dryer."

"A hair dryer?" I say, trying to hide my disappointment. I have one of those at home. Mom usually has to chase me around the apartment before I let her use it on me after a shower.

He laughs. "No, an *air* dryer. We use it to make repairs underwater. It allows us to pull out objects that get stuck in a drain line. Seeing as you're already in your swimsuit, I figured this is something you might like."

"Are you sure he should take this?" Dad asks. "It looks expensive."

"No worries," Graff says. "We've got plenty of 'em."

"Thanks!" I tell him, gripping it tight. A gadget of my very own! And it won't dry my hair!

Graff gives Pockets a little scratch on the top of his head and says, "Be well, my friend."

If anyone had told me a week ago that it would seem normal that a giant ant-like creature would be lovingly petting an over-size talking cat, I'd have told them they were nuts. Welcome to life in outer space!

Pockets is in a hurry to get to the water planet, but not in enough of a hurry to miss out on tuna at Barney's Bagels and Schmear. Dad tries to convince him we should get moving, but he pretends not to hear. We have no choice but to go with him. Truth be told, a bagel really does sound good.

Pockets plunks his money on the counter. "Three tuna bagel sandwiches," he says. "Heavy on the tuna."

"I was actually going to get cream cheese on mine," I tell Pockets.

"Oh, I wasn't ordering for you," he replies, licking his lips. "These are all for me."

Dad orders for the two of us and I follow

Pockets to a table. He digs into his lunch while I look around, trying to find the differences between this Barney's and the one not too far from our apartment on Earth.

For one thing, ours doesn't have a view of the Milky Way outside its window. And the guy behind the counter at home doesn't have six tentacles or three eyes. Or if he does, he did a really great job hiding it that one time I saw him. This Barney's is packed, just like the bagel shop at home. Only this one is full of aliens of all shapes and sizes and colors. Dad joins us and catches me staring. He gives me a disapproving look. I turn my attention to my food. Who could blame me if I peek every few seconds at a square-shaped alien at the next table? His mouth opens so wide he can (and does) stuff his whole sandwich in it.

"Is this seat taken?" a small voice asks.

I turn around to see a tiny red alien with one large eye in the center of his round face. Two long tentacles sway back and forth on the top of his head, like windshield wipers. He's holding a tray of food, and for some reason he looks kind of familiar. He clears his throat and asks again if the seat is taken.

"No," Dad and I say, quickly scooting down on the bench to make room.

"Yes," Pockets says, barely glancing up from his sandwich. "Sorry."

The alien's little tentacles droop and he hurries away, bent over his tray.

"That was rude, Pockets," Dad says. "There's plenty of room."

"And he was so cute," I add. "Like a little stuffed animal, but real."

Pockets licks the last bits of tuna off his paws and stands up. "Trust me, looks can be deceiving out here."

I try to see where the little red guy went, but I don't spot him anywhere in the restaurant. I could stay here all day just alien watching, but now that Pockets has eaten his tuna, he hurries us out.

Graff gassed up the taxi earlier, so we are soon zooming away from Akbar's Floating Rest Stop. According to my map, the only tricky part of the rest of the journey should be avoiding an asteroid that is very close to Nautilus. The big chunk of floating rock is only fifty miles across, which isn't big enough to give it much gravitational pull. So it shouldn't pull us toward it, but it can definitely crush us if we hit it. Or it hits us. Either way, it would be bad.

It doesn't take long until we enter the water planet's solar system. Just like the map warned, the asteroid is here. We are all silent as the huge chunk of space rock zooms by the taxi's rear window a little too close for comfort. The taxi bumps and jumps for a minute in the wake of the asteroid, then settles back down.

Soon we've reached the planet's atmosphere. "Deploy reverse thrusters," I tell Dad.

"Roger that," he says. But before he gets a chance, a huge, gushing wall of water appears out of nowhere and blocks our way.

That was definitely NOT on my map!

Chapter Five:
The Underwater Planet

"It's the water leaving Nautilus," Pockets shouts above the roar. "You will have to go above it."

"I can't," Dad shouts back, swerving left, then right. "The gravity from the planet is too strong at this point. It's pulling us toward it."

Then, just as suddenly as it appeared, the huge spout of water is gone. A few large drops splash against our windshield, and then all is quiet.

"That was weird," I say when my heart stops pounding. "Why is the water doing that?"

"That's what we're here to find out," Pockets says, almost cheerfully. He likes mysteries, too.

A thick, dark cloud hovers over most of Nautilus. It's not until the taxi flies below it that I can see why they call Nautilus a water planet.

Almost the entire surface is covered in water. I've never been to the ocean on Earth before, but this must be what it's like, only times a *hundred*. The water is an amazing light green color. I wonder what it would be like to swim in it! I know we're here on a mission, but it would be a shame to let my bathing suit go to waste.

"How about that one, Archie?" Dad asks. He's pointing at a circle of tiny islands connected by long silver bridges.

I don't even need to look down at my map. "Sorry, Dad. None of the islands have runways nearly long enough to land on."

"I figured," Dad says, gritting his teeth. "Let's hope this new landing gear works." He presses the new blue button on the dashboard. We wait. I don't hear anything.

"Did the skis come out underneath?" I ask, pressing my face up to my window.

Pockets scrambles to the other window. "I don't see anything," he reports.

"And there's no time to deploy my hot-air balloon."

I twist around. "You have a hot-air balloon?"

"Actually, I have two," he says. "I'll show you someday. Unless of course the taxi is smashed to bits when it hits the water. Then you'll just have to take my word for it."

I gulp.

"Hang on, boys, here we go," Dad says as the front of the taxi becomes level with the planet. He grips the steering wheel so tight his knuckles turn white. I hold my breath as the taxi skims across the surface of the water. We wobble back and forth, with first the front and then the back of the cab dipping underneath the water. Finally the taxi steadies itself and we start gently floating on the ripples toward the group of islands.

"Phew," Dad says, unpeeling his fingers from the wheel.

"Phew," Pockets and I agree.

"Wow, look!" I shout, rolling down my window. The water is so clear that I can see straight down to the ocean floor. I see round buildings and long sidewalks and so many people! Some are walking—more like gliding, really—while most are swimming. Some are even riding three-wheeled bicycles on the ocean floor.

"Wow," Pockets says, going from window to window in the backseat to get the best view.

"Wow," Dad agrees, sticking his head out his own window.

A group of people wave from a dock on the largest island. They rush to meet us as we pull in. Tall and thin, with fins instead of hands, they look more like fish than people. I'm not scared of them, though, like I was of Graff at first. After all, unlike the ants in kindergarten, Mom's never had to pull *fish* from my hair. That would be really, really gross.

They use a rope to tie us to the dock, then help us out of the car. Pockets flips open his official ISF badge and then introduces Dad and me.

"We are so glad you're here," a fish-person in a long blue robe with wide sleeves says. He bends way down to shake our hands. His fin-like hand is cold and clammy, but not in a bad way.

"I am Carp," he says. "I am the leader of the undersea people."

A woman in a green robe steps up next to him and shakes our hands, too. Her hand is much warmer, and a bit less fin-like. "And I am Salmon," she says, "leader of the abovesea people."

Carp turns to Pockets and says, "Salmon and I will fill you in on our current situation. Meanwhile, my son, Pike, will be happy to entertain the earthlings with a tour."

"Oh, I get it," I say with a grin. "Everyone here is named after a fish!"

"What do you mean?" Carp asks.

Pockets gives me a quick shake of his head.

"Never mind," I mutter, my cheeks growing hot.

Pike steps out from behind his father. He's like a mini version of his dad. I guess I must look like a mini version of *my* dad, too.

I lean over and whisper to Dad, "Shouldn't we stay with Pockets? How can we help him if we're not together?"

"He'll let us know if he needs us," Dad replies.

Pockets turns and motions for us to go with Pike. He and the two leaders hurry toward a nearby table.

"Come," Pike says, grabbing my hand in his cold one. "Let's go have fun!" He pulls me away from the dock and onto a grassy area. Dad glances back at our taxi bobbing in the water, seems satisfied that it's safe, and follows.

Pike points out the houses in the center

of the island. They look like they are made of dried-out mud. Colorful flowers and plants bloom everywhere and make the homes look cozy and inviting.

"Why do some people live up here, and some in the water?" I ask Pike.

"We all used to live undersea," he explains, climbing onto a large pile of moss-covered rocks. Dad and I step where he steps, being careful not to slip.

When we reach the top, he continues his story. "A few hundred years ago, people started exploring above. And now it has become home to many. If the oceans continue to dry up, then everyone will have to live above the water. Most of our bodies are not prepared for that. We do not breathe air well enough to live here full-time."

He kind of sounds like Pockets when he talks—all grown-up, even though he's still a kid. But then he suddenly does a backflip, stretches out his fin-like arms, and shouts, "Long live Nautilus!" No way Pockets would—or could—do *that*. Not that I could do it, either. I can't even do a somersault.

I clap and Pike grins, puffing out the gills on his cheeks.

"Very impressive," Dad says.

"One day I will be leader of the undersea," Pike says. "If there is an undersea left, that is. You are not visiting us at our best time." He points up at the huge cloud we flew past on our way here. It blocks most of the sun. "That cloud began to form when the water started disappearing," he says. "Usually our planet is sunny and warm."

"What do you think is making the water go away?" I ask.

His eyes dim. "Some undersea people think the abovesea people are behind it."

"But why would they want to get rid of the water?"

The gills on his face flap as he frowns. "If the water goes away, then everything undersea will be abovesea. Instead of only having a few islands to live on, they'll have the whole planet." His eyes get wet with tears. "And the rest of us won't be able to breathe."

"Do you really think they'd do that?" I ask. "Salmon seemed really nice. She's the leader of the abovesea people, right?"

Pike nods. "I don't really think they would do it. Neither does my father. But that's why the ISF officer is here, to help figure it out." He grins. "Come, let's forget our troubles for a moment. I want to show you my favorite place abovesea."

He leads us down the other side of the rocks and around to a hidden sandy cove. Two fish-men in uniforms sit on lifeguard stands on either side of the small beach.

"Do the lifeguards mean we can swim here?" I ask as we make our way toward the water. I spread my arms to show off my swimsuit. "I came prepared."

Pike laughs but shakes his head. "I'm sorry. But until we figure out what's happening with the water, swimming up here on the surface has been banned. And these men aren't lifeguards. They are guarding the entrance to the Nautilus National Bank below us."

One of the guards leans back in his chair and closes his eyes. The other pulls out a book to read.

"The bank hasn't been robbed in fifty years," Pike explains. "So they're pretty bored. People don't last too long at this job. These guys have only been here a few—"

A roaring *whoosh* drowns out the rest of his words. A steady stream of water races from the ocean right up to the sky, like an upside-down waterfall. The force of it pushes me and Pike backward onto the beach, but Dad is standing by the shoreline and falls the other way, right into the shallow water! By the time we scramble to our feet and reach him, the huge plume of water has disappeared, leaving the ocean as calm as ever.

Dad sits upright in the wet sand, water lapping at his waist.

"Are you all right, Mr. Morningstar?" Pike asks, bending down.

Dad looks up at us. Surprise and delight

THiS **WATER** SURE iS REFRESHiNG!

shine on his face. "This is the most refreshing water I've ever felt!" he says. Then he looks down at his wrist. "Oops, I got my watch wet." He peers closer at it. "Hey, it still works!"

Pike nods. "Our water is truly something special."

I am TOTALLY wishing I'd fallen in, too. I could slip while helping Dad stand up. Accidentally, of course. Then if I splashed around while trying to get out, that wouldn't be considered swimming, right? I'm about to put my plan into action, when Pockets comes running onto the beach, followed by a breathless Salmon and Carp.

"We must get back to the taxi!" Pockets shouts. "The bank has just been robbed!"

Chapter Six:
Under the Sea

We race back to the dock and pile into the taxi. "Follow us," Salmon says. She and Carp and Pike dive below the clear surface.

"Let's see what this baby can do underwater," Dad says, flicking a switch on the dashboard. I hold on tight as the sides of the taxi stretch out while the front flattens into the shape of a duck's bill. Instead of the rocket boosters that normally come out of the back of the taxi when we take off, propellers pop up and push the taxi down through the water. The wings move up and down now, like fins!

"That Graff does fine work," Dad says, leaning back in his seat as we go deeper.

"He does indeed," Pocket agrees. "But I am fairly certain *that's* not supposed to happen." He points to the rear window behind him. A thin crack has started to form down the middle.

Dad gulps loudly. "If the water pressure gets much stronger," he warns, "that window will break and the car could spin out of control."

My eyes widen. That doesn't sound good. Meanwhile, we keep going lower and the crack keeps growing. "We'd better warn the others," Dad says.

I look all around but don't see anyone. "The bubbles from the propellers are blocking them," I tell Dad.

"Hopefully, they are safely out of the way," he replies. "Graff warned us he didn't know how deep we could go before the water pressure would crush the car. I wish we knew how far we are from the ocean floor."

Pockets taps his paw against his chin, deep in thought. Then he says, "If only we had a copilot with a map to guide our way underwater…"

Yeah, that *would* be helpful. Oh, wait!

He means me! I quickly grab my map and pull it out of its tube. I'm not sure it will show us what's under the water, but it's worth a try.

It works! Instead of suns and planets and wormholes popping up in the air in front of me, I can see tunnels and buildings not too far below us, and reefs made of jagged rock and sand. Speaking of reefs! "Turn right, Dad!" I shout. "Reef wall directly in front of us!"

Dad veers quickly to the right. The edge of the left propeller clips the reef, but it doesn't look too serious. We're still in one piece.

"Good timing, Archie," he says when we level out. He shuts off the propellers and I glance behind us at the rear window, fearing the worst. But the crack doesn't look any worse. In fact, it looks...better? I'm about to ask how that's possible, when I see Pockets slip a tube of something into a pocket.

"Super-extra-special ISF glue," he says when he sees me looking.

"You could have mentioned you had that," I reply.

"I could have," Pockets admits. "But you need to learn how to handle dangerous situations. That's what will make you a better ISF deputy."

I'm about to argue that we are supposed to be a team, but I really *do* want to be the best deputy I can be. So I mutter something that would probably get me in trouble if anyone heard, and I turn back around. Without the bubbles from the propellers, I easily spot Carp and Salmon swimming up ahead. Pike swims up to my window, worry all over his face. He must have seen our near miss with the reef wall.

I give him a thumbs-up.

"There it is," Pockets says. "The Nautilus National Bank." We glide toward a huge white building with a silver dome on the top. Carp and Salmon wave us into an open garage.

A metal door lowers and seals us in. The water level in the garage slowly gets lower and lower as the water is sucked down a big drain on the floor. When only puddles are left on the floor, we open the doors.

Pockets hops out first, a huge grin on his face. "Guess what?" he asks.

"We made it without being crushed or crashing?" I say.

"Well, yes, that," he says. "But guess who's underwater without a drop of water on him? Me!" He beams with delight.

I shake my head. That cat *really* doesn't like water.

A door swings open at the far end of the garage. Pike runs through it to greet us. "I am so glad you made it safely, Archie," he says. "That looked pretty scary."

"It was the taxi's first time underwater," I admit. "But the three of us are a good team."

Dad pats me on the shoulder as we all walk into the bank. Broken tiles and bricks lie in piles on the floor, but other than that, the bank looks pretty much like a regular bank. Lots of thick marble walls, shiny floors, and big doors with big locks.

Carp hurries up to Pockets and says, "It appears the alarm went off before the robbers could complete the tunnel they were digging. We don't yet know whether anything was stolen or not. The abovesea people are blaming the undersea people, and the undersea people are blaming those above. Salmon is trying to keep the peace, but it's a mess!"

Pockets pulls out a yellow pencil from a small pocket under his arm. "Never fear," he says. "The ISF is here."

I'm about to tell Pockets he made a rhyme, but he's in his official ISF officer mode and probably wouldn't appreciate the teasing right now.

I figure he's going to pull out a notebook next, but he doesn't. Instead he presses down on the pencil's eraser and the biggest magnifying glass I've ever seen pops out. He holds it up in front of his face. Pike and I laugh. "You should see how big your nose looks!" I tell him.

"And your whiskers!" Pike adds.

Pockets moves the magnifying glass forward and back so his nose gets really big and long. Pike and I crack up. Then Pockets glances at Carp and quickly puts his serious expression back on. "This will help me find any clues the robbers left behind," he explains to everyone. "And they always leave clues behind."

"You'll need to start outside," Carp says. "Before any evidence gets washed away."

"Outside?" Pockets asks. His eyes begin to dart around the room, like he's looking for an escape. "Outside in the *water*, you mean?"

"Of course," Carp says. "The robbers broke in from outside. Any clues would be there. If we're not too late already."

Pockets is clearly frozen with fear. I'm not even sure he's breathing. Only his eyes are moving. I've never seen him look like this. I'm not sure what to do. Suddenly I *do* know. We're a team. Sure, Pockets is the leader when we're on missions, but we help each other out. I step forward. "I'll go," I tell Carp. "You need Pockets here on the inside. Someone has to keep the peace between the two sides. He's really good at that."

Carp looks unsure, but then Dad steps forward. "I'll go, too," he offers. "Four eyes are better than two."

"Make that *six* eyes," Pike says, joining us. "They'll need someone to show them around."

Carp nods. "Fine. Let's get moving."

Pockets finally takes a breath. He reaches out to squeeze my hand with his paw. Then he whips out what look like plastic fishbowls and hands one to me and one to Dad. "These helmets will let you breathe underwater for a half hour," he explains.

Dad and I slip the helmets over our

heads. They instantly seal around our shoulders. Cool!

Pockets pulls us into a huddle, including Pike. "Keep your eyes open for anything unusual," he says.

"How will we know what's unusual?" I ask. "There's a city under the ocean. Everything is unusual."

Pockets considers this. "Good point. Each crime scene is different, of course, but one rule is always the same: You need to look for something that seems out of place, like it doesn't belong there."

Pockets looks from me to Dad. "This is good practice for Intergalactic Security Force deputies." He pats us on the back and hurries off with his huge magnifying glass pencil.

"You'll get to see how we keep the bank dry," Pike says. "It's pretty cool." He leads Dad and me to a nearby hole in the wall. I'd thought this was part of the damage from the robbery, but clearly it's meant to be here. It's dry when we step inside it, but it slopes downward, slowly filling with water until we can swim right out.

"Definitely cool," I agree, spreading my arms and lifting off the ground.

Dad was right—this water is amazing. It's almost crackling with energy. It feels thicker than the water at home, almost like I'm swimming through syrup. No... it's not really sticky like that, more like pudding. Penny would love it, since she loves anything to do with pudding. Suddenly,

Penny and Mom feel really far away and I get a pang of homesickness. Then I remind myself that I'm getting to swim deep underwater on another planet and I know Mom would want me to enjoy it.

I follow Pike around to the back of the bank, where we spot a huge hole almost as big as the bank itself. Piled on all sides of the hole are equally huge mounds of sand mixed with shiny black rocks that must have come out of the ocean floor.

Dad motions that he'll take a closer look on one side and I should take the other. I swim around to the smallest pile and start looking. Mostly I see sand. A lot of sand and a lot of rocks. The shiny rocks are very pretty. I reach for one the size of a golf ball and try to pull it off the pile to bring home for Penny. Only it won't come off. I try a different one. It moves a little but snaps right back into place. They're all stuck to one another, like magnets!

I'm about to give up, when I remember the air-dryer gadget Graff gave me back

at the garage. I pull it out of the pocket of my swim shorts and push the end with the suction cup against the pile of rocks. One flick of a switch later and a small rock bursts free of the pile and shoots inside the tube. A little cover slides over the top, sealing it in.

I grin. That was easy! I try to slide the gadget back into my pocket, but it misses and drops slowly to the ocean floor. When I bend to pick it up, a small metal object in the sand catches my eye. It's a screwdriver! My first clue as an ISF deputy! What a rush!

My heart beating fast, I grab it with both hands.

Only I can't make it budge at all. I wave my arms in the water and call out, "Guys!

Come see what I found!" I'm not sure they can hear me through the fishbowl on my head, but my splashing around gets their attention. I grab hold of the tool while Dad and Pike tug on my arms. It takes all three of us yanking REALLY HARD to pull it free from the large rocks. I open up the air dryer and drop the screwdriver inside to keep it safe. As I tighten the cap, I realize I could have used it to pull the screwdriver free from the magnetized rocks. Oops!

We keep searching the area but don't see anything else out of the ordinary. Dad points to his helmet and then to his watch. We're almost out of breathing time.

We swim back through the tunnel until swimming turns to walking and we're inside again. We yank off our helmets and hurry over to Pockets and Carp. I unscrew the top of my air dryer and flip it over while Dad describes the huge hole.

The small rock falls out into my palm first, followed by the screwdriver, which is stuck to the end of the rock. "Could this be something?" I ask, prying them apart and handing Pockets the tool.

Pockets holds his giant magnifying glass up to it and lets out a sharp meow. "It sure is something!" he shouts, pointing to the edge. With the magnifying glass we can clearly read the words PROPERTY OF B.U.R.P.

B.U.R.P.? The biggest, baddest group of criminals in the universe is involved in this? I'm so surprised that I drop the black rock. It clatters noisily to the marble floor.

Two things happen really fast after that. Pockets shouts, "Whoa!" and the screwdriver flies out of his paw, over Pike's head, and into my hand.

Chapter Seven:
A Postcard Would've Been Nice

"What just happened?" Dad asks as I struggle to peel the screwdriver from my palm. It takes some effort, but finally I'm able to push it into Pockets's paw. He grasps it tight this time.

"It was the stone," Carp says. "It is not supposed to reach the air."

The rock has rolled between Dad's feet. "This little rock?" he asks, bending over to pick it up.

"Don't!" Carp says, stepping between Dad and the rock. "Over the centuries the people of Nautilus have adapted to the strongly magnetic mineral that is found under our ocean floor. It has no effect on us. But when visitors to our planet come in contact with it when the stone is dry, *they* become magnetic."

Dad backs away from the rock and pulls me close to him. "Is it dangerous?" he asks, his voice tight.

Carp shakes his head. "He only touched it with one hand. He'll be fine in a few days. A few weeks at most."

"I'm sorry, Dad," I say. "I thought it would be a cool gift for Penny."

He sighs. "Maybe next time just get her a postcard."

Pockets pulls a square coin out of his pocket and tosses it at me. It lands right in the palm of my hand without me even reaching for it. Cool! I peel the alien coin off my hand and slip it in my pocket.

I'm not sure I mind being magnetic if it means I get to pick up stray coins from different planets. I might even start a collection!

"Hey!" Pockets says. His tail starts swishing back and forth like windshield wipers.

"Okay, okay," I say, reaching into my pocket for the coin. "I'll give it back."

"No, it's not that," Pockets says quickly. "I've just realized I know what B.U.R.P. was doing down here. And they weren't robbing the bank."

"Sure looks like it," Carp says.

Pockets shakes his head. "I believe they want what is buried under the ocean floor—the rocks! And judging by the size of the hole, they want a LOT of them.

The digging must have set off the bank alarms."

"If that's true," Salmon says, "then where are all the rocks? There's nowhere to hide them."

I look down at my small rock, still lying on the floor. If I hadn't taken it, I wouldn't have found the screwdriver, and Pockets wouldn't have figured out what B.U.R.P. was after. Strange how one thing leads to another. Suddenly, the pieces come together like a puzzle. "It's the water," I blurt out.

"*What's* the water, Archie?" Dad asks.

"That's how they're getting the mineral off the planet," I explain. "It's like when me and Penny play at the pool, you know, with that water jet, and it's so strong it pushes our hands away? Couldn't those really powerful gushes of water be bringing the rocks up to the sky?"

Pockets claps his paws together. "The boy is absolutely right! B.U.R.P. has been grinding up the rocks and then setting off the waterspouts to send the magnetic material right up to the sky. It's a brilliant plot!"

Carp and Salmon stare with wide eyes at Pockets, then turn to face each other. "I am so ashamed," Carp says. "We were blaming each other when it was B.U.R.P. taking our water all along."

"Not our finest moment," Salmon agrees. "I am sorry, too."

The two leaders shake hands warmly.

"And the good news is that the water

and the rocks are still here," Pockets says, "inside that huge cloud. They haven't gotten away with it."

Pike rushes in from the other room. "Everyone! Come quick! The cloud is moving!"

Chapter Eight:
A Sticky Situation

Between me worrying about avoiding the reef wall and Pockets worrying about being too late to catch B.U.R.P., the ride up to the surface is not much fun. We finally reach the dock and scramble out of the taxi. I shiver. The cloud is even bigger now, after the last spout, and it completely blocks the sun.

Abovesea and undersea people huddle together on the island. Many are looking up at the huge cloud, but others are still talking about the bank robbery. The two guards we saw earlier at the beach are trying to keep everyone calm, but it doesn't seem to be working very well.

The cloud is moving slowly, but it's definitely moving. It also seems to have started humming. That's not something you usually hear from clouds. In fact, you usually don't hear *anything* from clouds. I mean, except for thunder, of course. But thunder doesn't hum. At least it doesn't on Earth.

"Does the cloud usually hum?" I ask Pike.

"I've never heard that sound before," he says, moving noticeably closer to his dad.

Pockets whips out a pair of the biggest binoculars I've ever seen.

"It's the engines of a spaceship!" he declares. "It's pulling the cloud!"

The crowd gasps.

"Are we going after it?" I ask, already plotting out the route in my head.

He shakes his head. "By the time we got up there, whoever is in that ship would be on the other side of the galaxy. I have a better idea." He stashes the binoculars away and pulls out a long gold-colored tube. It looks a little like the tube I stash my space map in, only this one is wider and longer and not black with a silver star on it. He holds it up. "My trusty new Flirbin Blaster is going to fix things right up."

I'm about to ask what it does, but Pockets is busy fishing around for something else. He finally pulls out a rain poncho. In one motion, he slips it over his head. Then he aims the Flirbin Blaster at the cloud and twists the bottom. Instantly, a stream of something white shoots straight into the sky. Little bits of it waft down onto my back and neck. "Ow, that's COLD!" I begin to shiver.

"The Flirbin Blaster shoots dry ice," Pockets explains. He keeps it aimed at the cloud.

"Dry ice?" I repeat. "Like what the doctor uses to burn off a wart?" I personally haven't had experience with this, but Dad's always coming home from work with weird things on his body. He must be

picking up germs from the planets he visits on his route. I have a feeling I'm going to be taking a lot more baths from now on.

"Well, yes," Pockets says impatiently. "I suppose you could use it for wart removal."

"And it looks cool at parties," Dad adds. "Like you're dancing on a fluffy white cloud."

"But how will it help us now?" I ask, having trouble picturing my dad dancing on a regular floor, let alone a cloud.

Instead of answering, Pockets tosses ponchos to Dad and me. "Quick, put these on. Make sure you are completely covered."

No sooner do I flip up my hood and thrust my hands into the pockets than it begins to rain. Slowly at first, and then the drops fall faster and faster until everyone around us is soaked. Tiny fragments of black rock stick to my poncho, like pulp in fresh-squeezed orange juice.

Finally the rain stops, and for the first time since we've been on Nautilus, the sun comes out, and with it, the heat. Pockets wiggles out of his poncho and tosses it aside. I notice he's careful not to touch the outside. Dad and I do the same.

"Where'd the spaceship go?" Pike asks, shielding his eyes as he searches the sky.

Carp frowns. "Now we will never know how they were able to get into our oceans without anyone seeing them. As you can tell by looking at us, someone from another planet would certainly stand out."

"Unless they wore disguises so that they could blend in," Pockets says, grinning.

He rushes over to the crowd. We all share a puzzled look but hurry after him.

There's some big commotion in the center of the group. Pockets pushes his way through and then announces, "Aha! Gotcha!" He does a backflip right over a picnic bench (guess I was wrong about him being able to do that!) and tackles two men to the ground. I stare down in surprise as I recognize the uniforms the men are wearing.

"No, Pockets," I shout. "Those are the guards from the beach. They're not from B.U.R.P."

"Really?" Pockets asks. "Then explain *this*." He flips both the men over (truly, he is very strong for a cat), and we all gasp. Up close, I can see that the guards' hands are plastic gloves painted to *look* like real fins! These men aren't from Nautilus at all! Every spot that isn't covered by their uniforms is covered in something metal. Coins, spoons, keys, paper clips.

One of the guards even has a frying pan stuck to his arm!

I look back up at Pockets, who is standing over the magnetized guards, grinning proudly. I realize now that this was part of his plan all along. Making it rain would not only return the water and the mineral to Nautilus—it would reveal the bad guys as soon as the mineral dried on their skin. That Pockets is one smart cat!

The guards try to stand up, but Salmon and Carp spring into action and hold them firmly in place.

Pockets holds up his badge. "I am Intergalactic Security Force officer Pilarbing Fangorious Catapolitus," he tells the guards. "Otherwise known as Pockets." He winks at me before turning back to the guards. "You are under arrest for helping B.U.R.P. steal minerals from beneath the ocean floor of the planet Nautilus."

Before the guards can argue, Pockets's badge flies out of his hand and sticks to one of the guard's cheeks. Pockets leans over and peels it off. "I'll take that back, thank you very much."

The guards grumble angrily. I quietly unstick a paper clip from my hand. No need to remind everyone that I have something in common with the criminals.

"Looks like your friend up there has ditched you," Pockets tells them, waving at the sky. "But the ISF will be happy to give you a ride off the planet. Your plan to steal the mineral is foiled."

One of the guards grunts. "The mineral

was just the start," he says. "We were going to make a giant magnet and drag the asteroid away."

The other guard kicks his friend in the shin. "Don't tell them anything!"

Dad and I look at each other in surprise. The *asteroid*? The one we dodged on the way here? Pockets must be surprised, too, but he doesn't show it. In a flash, he has both guards handcuffed and tied together.

"B.U.R.P. will find another way to steal an asteroid—just you wait," the first guard snarls, trying unsuccessfully to pull at the knots around his arms. The second guard goes to kick him again and the metal tip of his boot gets stuck to the first guard's knee.

It's hard not to laugh.

Salmon and a bunch of other abovesea

people form a circle around the guards while Carp and Pike walk us to our taxi.

"What do you think they were planning to do with the asteroid?" Pike asks Pockets. He's been staring at him in awe ever since Pockets single-handedly took down the criminals.

Pockets thinks for a moment. "If they could control an asteroid, they could do a lot of damage to any planet in their path."

"An asteroid landing on my planet wiped out all the dinosaurs," I tell Pike. "And the dinosaurs were REALLY big and had been there for a long time."

"Let's hope B.U.R.P. gave up their plans," Carp says, putting his hand on his son's shoulder. To the rest of us he says, "We can't thank you enough for all you've done. After the rain, the ocean is back to its normal level now. And just as important, our people are again united."

Pockets tips an imaginary hat at them. "Just doing my job," he says. Then he puts his paws around me and Dad and adds, "We're just doing *our* job, I mean."

Pockets climbs into the backseat first, springing easily over the gap between the dock and the taxi. He reaches into a pocket and pulls out his pillow and what looks like an ordinary sheet. But when he pulls it over himself, he completely blends into the seat! Other than a vague cat-shaped spot, I can't see him at all. Pike and I gasp.

"How are you doing that?" I ask.

"It's my camouflage blanket," he explains. "A very handy gadget for when I want to hide in plain sight. Or when I don't want to be bothered. It's been way too long since my last nap." And with that, he begins to snore.

Dad and I climb into the taxi a lot less gracefully than Pockets did. I don't need to bother to reach for the seat belt, since the end of it instantly flies into my hand. I have to pry it off in order to click it in place. I'm going to have to dig out my winter gloves when I get home, or the kids at school are gonna start asking questions when their lunch money flies out of their hands and sticks to mine! Although, then they'll think it's weird that I'm wearing gloves in school. Oh, well. No one said being an ISF deputy was going to be easy.

Pike stands at my door. "It was wonderful to meet you, Archie," he says. "I will never forget you."

"Me, either," I tell him. "Even after my hand returns to normal."

He laughs and waves good-bye. Then he walks to the edge of the dock and does a perfect dive into the ocean.

"I wish I could do that," I tell Dad.

"Maybe one day Pike will teach you," Dad replies, checking his mirrors.

"Really? Do you think I'll see him again?"

"It's possible, Archie. The universe may be a very big place, but good friends make it a lot smaller."

Dad twists the com line on. "Morning-star and son, setting a course for home."

"Is the cat with you?" the mouse asks.

Dad glances in the backseat. "Well, can't say as I see him right now. He sort of disappeared." Dad winks at me and I stifle a laugh.

"Just like a cat," the mouse scoffs. "Can't be trusted, I tell you."

Pockets growls.

"I thought you were asleep," I call back to him.

"I am," Pockets replies.

"Who is that?" the mouse asks. "Is that the cat? I told you he can't be—"

Dad and I laugh while Pockets hisses. "Morningstar out," Dad says, switching off the line. The taxi's engine roars to life, and we are on our way home.

I twist around in my seat one last time. Pike gives one final wave and then dives beneath the water's surface. I sit back and smile. The universe just became a little smaller.

THREE SCIENCE FACTS TO IMPRESS YOUR FRIENDS AND TEACHERS

1. Where do **CLOUDS** come from? When the sun warms up the air, water from oceans and lakes and rivers begins to evaporate. This means it turns into water vapor (a gas that you can't see) and begins to rise through the air. As the air gets cooler, the vapor sticks to dust in the atmosphere. Eventually the rising water vapor comes together to form a cloud. When the cloud grows heavy with water droplets and it can't hold any more, the water falls from the clouds and it begins to rain. Fog is a cloud that has formed at ground level.

2. A SUBMARINE (called a sub for short) is a large vessel that travels underwater. It is large enough for a crew of people to live inside it. Scientists use subs to explore beneath the ocean, and the navy uses them to help keep the oceans safe. Some can go as deep as eight hundred feet. A sub is also a kind of sandwich, but it would get very soggy underwater and no one would want to eat it. Except for Pockets, if it were a tuna sub.

3. MAGNETITE is a mineral found underground in parts of the world. This is where the word for *magnet* comes from. Magnets can push and pull on things with an invisible force by creating what is called a magnetic field. The magnetic field attracts certain metals like iron, nickel, and cobalt. Anything made out of these materials will stick to something magnetic.

WENDY MASS has written lots of books for kids. MICHAEL BRAWER is a teacher who drives space taxis on the side.  They live in New Jersey with their two kids and two cats, none of whom have left the solar system.

 ELISE GRAVEL has been drawing monsters and strange creatures for as long as she can remember. She's even raising two little space creatures of her own in Montreal, Canada, where she lives with her husband.

Don't miss a single **SPACE TAXI** adventure!

BOOK 1

BOOK 2

BOOK 3